Hello Kitty's
Snow Day, Hooray!

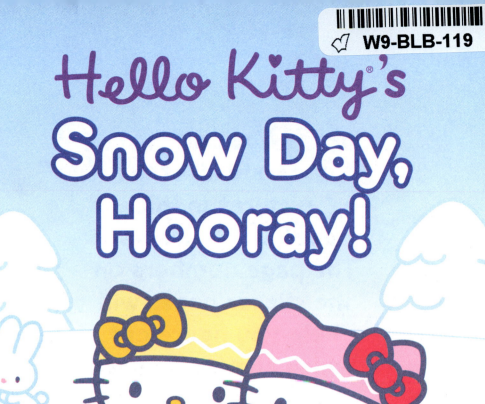

by Brian James
Illustrated by Sachiho Hino

SCHOLASTIC INC.

New York   Toronto   London   Auckland   Sydney
Mexico City   New Delhi   Hong Kong   Buenos Aires

You can
decorate all of the
pictures in this
book with stickers.
The page numbers on
the sticker pages will
help you figure out
which stickers to use.

ISBN-13: 978-0-545-00022-2
ISBN-10: 0-545-00022-X

Text and illustrations © 2008 SANRIO CO., LTD., USED UNDER LICENSE.
Character © 1976 SANRIO CO., LTD., USED UNDER LICENSE.

12 11 10 9 8 7 6 5 4 3 2 1   8 9 10 11 12 13/0

Printed in the U.S.A.
First printing, January 2008

Hello Kitty and Mimmy were very excited.
The big sled race was in one week.

It was a team race.
Hello Kitty and Mimmy were a team.

Papa helped them build a sled.
It was big enough for both of them.

Mimmy helped Papa cut the wood.
Hello Kitty helped Papa hammer nails.

"You are both very good helpers,"
Papa said.

Next the girls painted their sled.
They painted it red.
Then they painted pink flowers on it.

"It is very pretty," Mama said.
"It's the prettiest!" said Hello Kitty.
Hello Kitty was very proud of their sled.

The sled was finished.
There was only one thing missing.
SNOW!

"I hope it snows soon," Hello Kitty said.
"Me, too," said Mimmy.

Hello Kitty hoped for snow all week.
But by Friday, it still hadn't snowed.
Hello Kitty and her school friends
were sad.

They had worked hard on their sleds.
"If it doesn't snow tonight, there won't be
a race," Fifi said.

"We'll have to make a wish," Tippy said.
"I cross my fingers to make a wish,"
Joey said.
"I close my eyes to make a wish,"
said Kathy.

They made their wishes.

"I can't make my wish until tonight,"
Hello Kitty said.

She needed a star to make her wish.

That night, Hello Kitty looked out the window.
"I see a star," Mimmy said.

Hello Kitty and Mimmy each made a wish.
They wished for snow.

"Time for bed," Mama said.
Hello Kitty and Mimmy brushed their teeth.

Then they put on their pajamas.
They took one last look out the window.
There was still no snow.

In the morning, Hello Kitty woke up and looked outside.
Everything was white!
"Hooray!" she yelled.

It had snowed.
Hello Kitty and Mimmy ran downstairs to tell Papa.

"Papa! It snowed!" Hello Kitty shouted.
Papa smiled. He told the girls to get
ready for the race.

Hello Kitty and Mimmy put on their warmest clothes.
Then it was time to go.

Papa took the girls to the big hill.
Tippy, Fifi, Kathy, and Joey were there.

"Our wishes came true," Fifi said.
"That's because we all wished together,"
Hello Kitty said.

Hello Kitty and Mimmy sat on their sled.
Papa looked around at the other sleds
and frowned.
"Those sleds look fast," he said.

"It's okay if our sled doesn't win,"
Mimmy told him.
"We're happy just spending time with
you," Hello Kitty said.
Papa was very happy after that.

Soon, all the teams were ready.
It was time for the race to start.

"Get set! Go!" yelled the race judge.
Whoosh!

The girls raced downhill.
"Wheee!" Hello Kitty shouted.
"Yay!" yelled Mimmy.

When the race was over,
they had won third place.
They were very happy.

"Congratulations, Papa," Hello Kitty said.
"You're part of our team, too!" said Mimmy.
They gave Papa a big hug.
"Let's go home and celebrate," Papa said.
"Hooray!" the girls shouted.
Snow days were the best!